What's So Special About Today?

IT'S MY BIRTHDAY

by Jane Belk Moncure
illustrated by Jenny Williams

THE CHILD'S WORLD

ELGIN, ILLINOIS 60120

Distributed by Childrens Press,
Chicago, Illinois 60607.

Library of Congress Cataloging in Publication Data

Moncure, Jane Belk.
  What's so special about today? : it's my birthday / Jane Belk
Moncure ; illustrated by Jenny Williams.
     p.   cm. — (What's so special)

  Summary: Ben's fifth birthday is the most special day of his life,
as his presents include the puppy he wants very much.
  ISBN 0-89565-414-8
  [1. Birthdays—Fiction.   2. Dogs—Fiction.]   I. Williams, Jenny,
1939-   ill.   II. Title.   III. Series: Moncure, Jane Belk.   What's
so special.   87-21907
PZ7.M739Whgf   1987   CIP
[E]—dc 19   AC

1 2 3 4 5 6 7 8 9 10 11 12 R 96 95 94 93 92 91 90 89 88

What's So Special About Today?

IT'S MY BIRTHDAY

What's so special about today? It's my
birthday, that's what. The day started
out special . . .

when my sister made me a giant
birthday card. It was really neat!

Then for breakfast, Mom fixed pan-
cakes and put birthday candles on top.

I made a wish, but I didn't tell what it
was. Everyone knew my wish though.
Ever since I can remember, I've wished
for a puppy.

Later, Megan and I blew up balloons
for my birthday party and . . .

decorated the table. All the time I kept
thinking, "I hope Mom and Dad give
me a puppy."

Then my best friends came, and
everyone said, "Happy Birthday" . . .

and gave me presents . . . lots of
presents.

We had ice cream and cake. Just as I
blew out the candles, Dad came in
with a bundle in his arms.

"My puppy!" I thought. But Dad opened
it, and it was only a bundle of kites—one
for everyone.

My friends and I had fun flying the
kites! Then we played games and
giggled a lot. It was a special party.

When it was time to say good-by to my
friends, I thought the fun part of my
birthday was over.

But just then my grandparents came
with a big gift. I wanted to open it
right away.

But mom put the gift by the front door.
"Wait," she said. "We have a present
for you to open first."

She gave me a little box. When I saw
it, I thought, "No puppy this year."

Boy, was I surprised! In the box I found
a dog collar and a leash. There was a
note on the collar.

Guess what it said?

Happy Birthday, Ben!
This is a
Treasure Hunt.
A little brush,
found by you,
will lead the way
to clue number 2.

I dashed upstairs . . .

I looked on my dresser . . . nothing
there. Then . . .

I looked under my bed. I found socks,
a shoe, and a little blue brush.

Boy, was I excited. The brush had a
note on it too.

Guess what it said?

Find something that will bounce for me. That will lead you to clue number 3.

I knew right away it was a ball for my puppy. But where was it?

I looked in the toy box. It was not there. Then, I looked in my jacket pocket. I felt a lump. There it was— a ball for my puppy.

A note on the ball said:

Open the box by the front door, and you will find clue number 4

"My present from Grandma and Grandpa!" I shouted.

I dashed to the door and . . .

unwrapped the gift. It was a little dog-
house . . . with a note on it. I could
hardly wait to read the note.

It said:

Look for me
in a place
that is dark,
and you will
hear me bark.

There was only one dark place in our
house . . . the closet under the stairs.

I opened the door. . . and out jumped
a tiny cocker spaniel. He licked me
right in the face. "Wow!" I shouted.
"Thanks a lot . . . .

"Thanks a thousand times! I'll name him
Champ." And I did.

What's so special about today? It's my
birthday. I had a party, and my wish
came true. I think it's been the most
special day of my life.